18 Barcelona, *Spain*

19 Rome, *Italy*

20 Athens, *Greece*

21 Istanbul, *Turkey*

W9-BOL-675

26 Mumbai, *India*

27 Hong Kong, *China*

28 Beijing, *China*

29 Tokyo, *Japan*

30 Seoul, *South Korea*

31 Bangkok, *Thailand*

32 Jakarta, *Indonesia*

33 Sydney, *Australia*

34 Auckland, *New Zealand*

Benoit Tardif

METROPOLIS

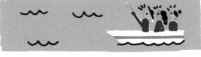

Kids Can Press

CONTENTS

LEGEND

 country   💬 language most spoken   👤 population of urban area

The world is filled with so many wonderful cities! As a boy, I wanted to visit them all — from New York to Paris to Tokyo, and everywhere in between. Then when I was older, I traveled to some of these places to see for myself what makes them so special.

In this book you will find many, but not all, of the world's greatest cities. They are all different, but they do have at least one thing in common: they are metropolises, or large and important cities.

Here you'll discover a few of the things you might see — and eat and do! — if you were to visit. I hope this book satisfies some of your curiosity about these faraway places and inspires you to explore them one day.

Bon voyage!

BENOIT

MONTREAL

Canada   French, English   4 million

Notre-Dame Basilica

Montreal-style bagel

BAGEL SHOP

BAGEL CHAUD AU FOUR À BOIS

3

Clock Tower

star hockey player

4

AAAAAAH

La Ronde amusement park

Palais des congrès (convention center)

Mount Royal

Tam-Tams festival

smoked meat sandwich

COLA

typical houses

talented musician

Olympic Stadium

Montreal Tower

funicular

5

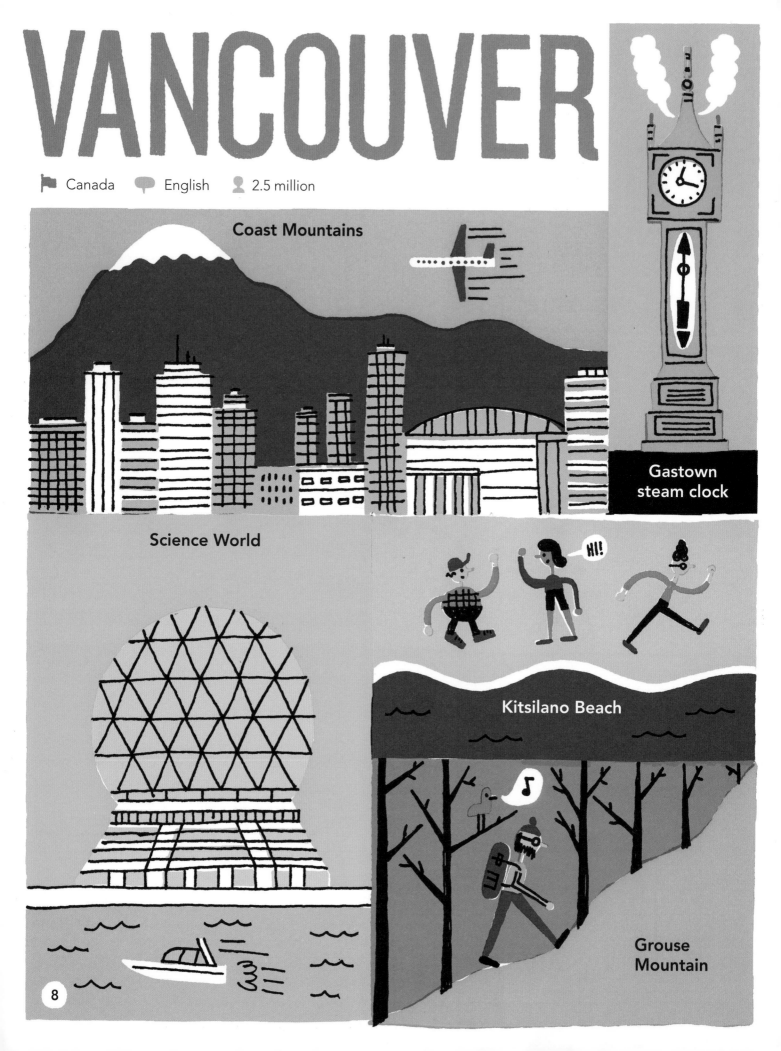

NEW YORK

🏳 United States of America 💬 English 👤 23.6 million

Empire State Building

Chrysler Building

baseball player on the lookout

HOT DOGS

hot dog stand

Guggenheim Museum (art gallery)

42nd Street traffic

CHICAGO

United States of America   English   9.9 million

Marina City twin towers

Buckingham Fountain

blues musician

Wrigley Building

Chicago River cruise

SAN FRANCISCO

🏳 United States of America 💬 English 👤 8.6 million

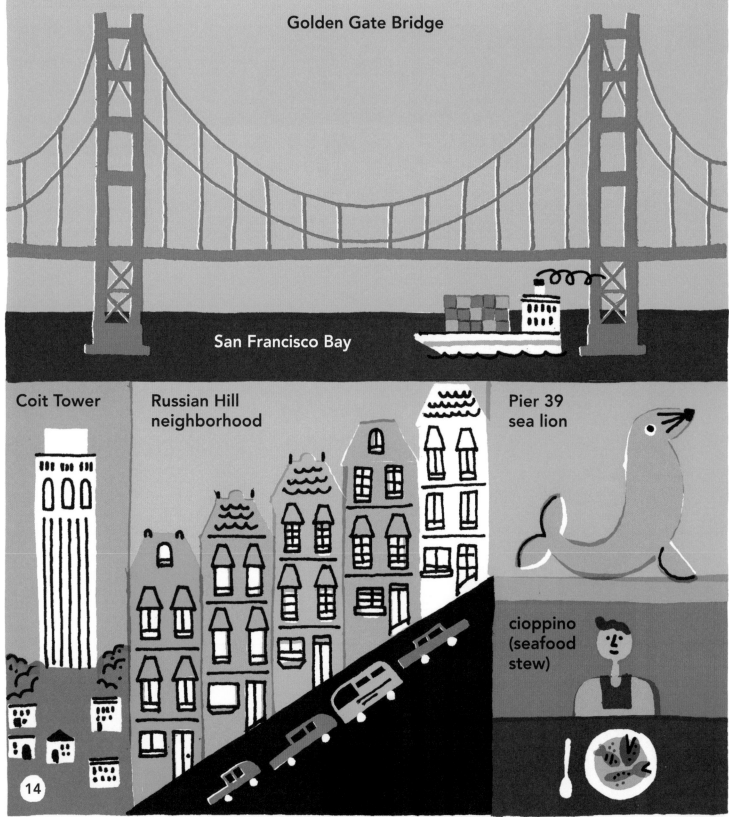

Golden Gate Bridge

San Francisco Bay

Coit Tower

Russian Hill neighborhood

Pier 39 sea lion

cioppino (seafood stew)

14

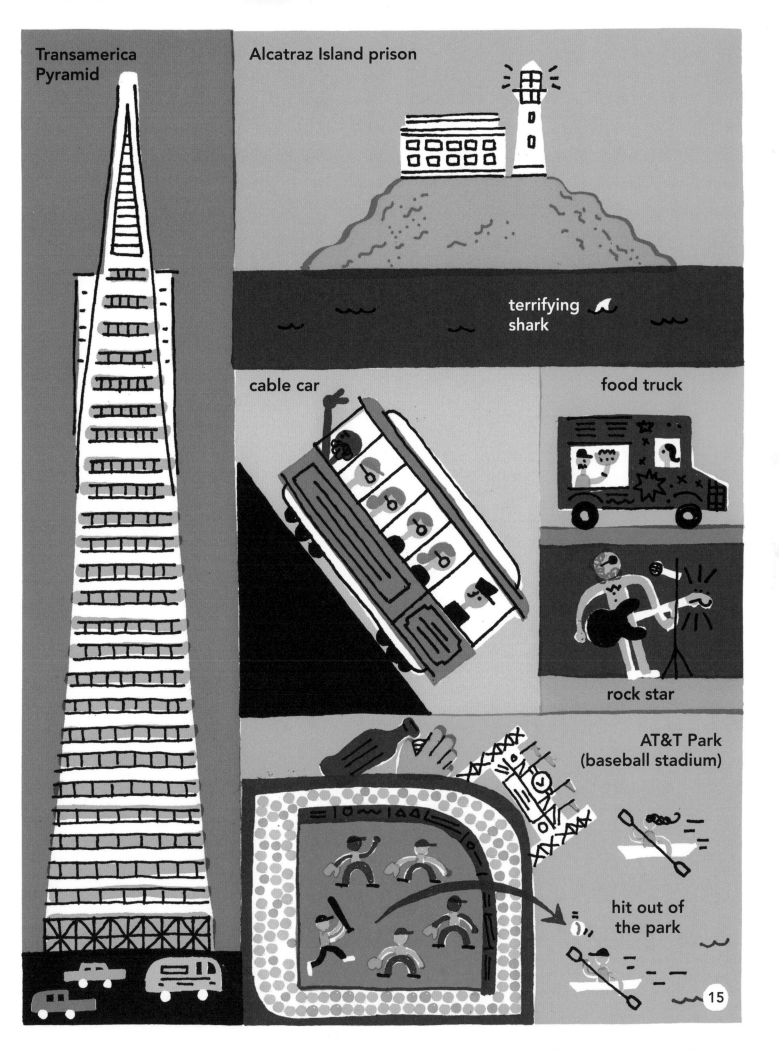

Transamerica Pyramid

Alcatraz Island prison

terrifying shark

cable car

food truck

rock star

AT&T Park (baseball stadium)

hit out of the park

15

MEXICO CITY

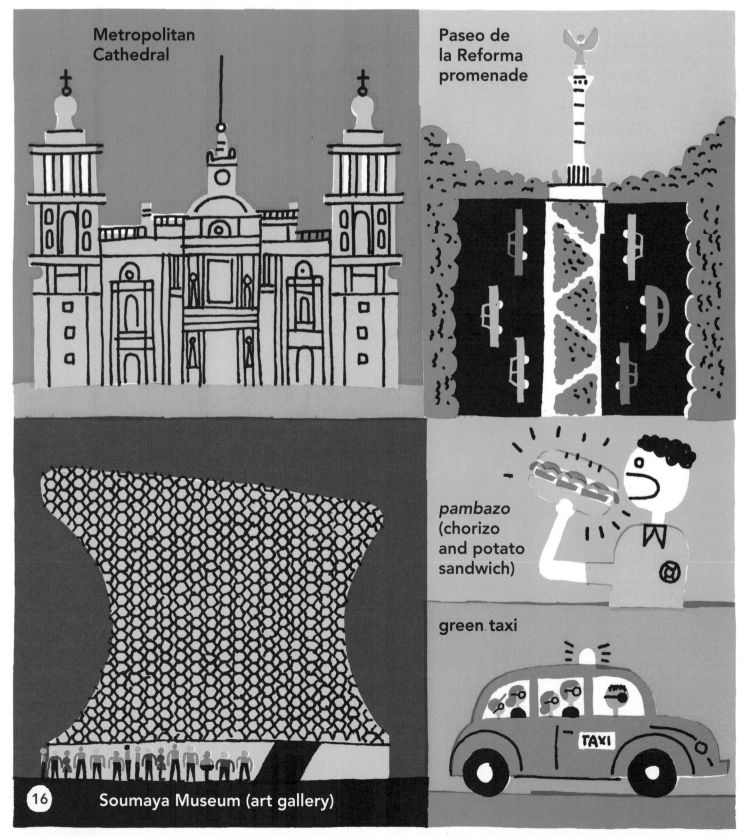

Metropolitan Cathedral

Paseo de la Reforma promenade

pambazo (chorizo and potato sandwich)

green taxi

16 Soumaya Museum (art gallery)

Popocatepetl and Iztaccihuatl volcanoes

Coyolxauhqui Stone showing Aztec moon goddess (Templo Mayor Museum)

Frida Kahlo Museum

MUSEO FRIDA KAHLO

caldo tlalpeño

ES PICANTE!

(chicken and chipotle soup)

Chapultepec Castle

Azteca Stadium (soccer)

17

Copacabana beach

Metropolitan Cathedral of Saint Sebastian

coconut water

Santa Teresa tram

LOVELY DAY AT THE BEACH

Atlantic Ocean

Rio Carnival costume

favela (shantytown)

19

BUENOS AIRES

🏴 Argentina   💬 Spanish   👤 14.2 million

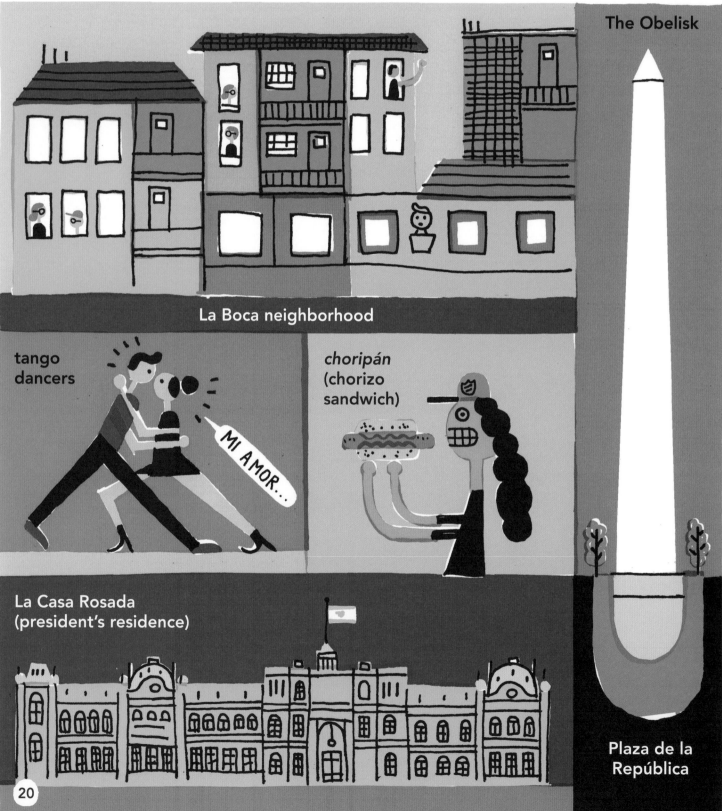

The Obelisk

La Boca neighborhood

tango dancers

MI AMOR...

choripán (chorizo sandwich)

La Casa Rosada (president's residence)

Plaza de la República

monument in La Recoleta Cemetery

Colón Theater (opera house)

Floralis Genérica sculpture

speedy soccer player

aquarium at the Buenos Aires Zoo

Women's Bridge in the Puerto Madero district

21

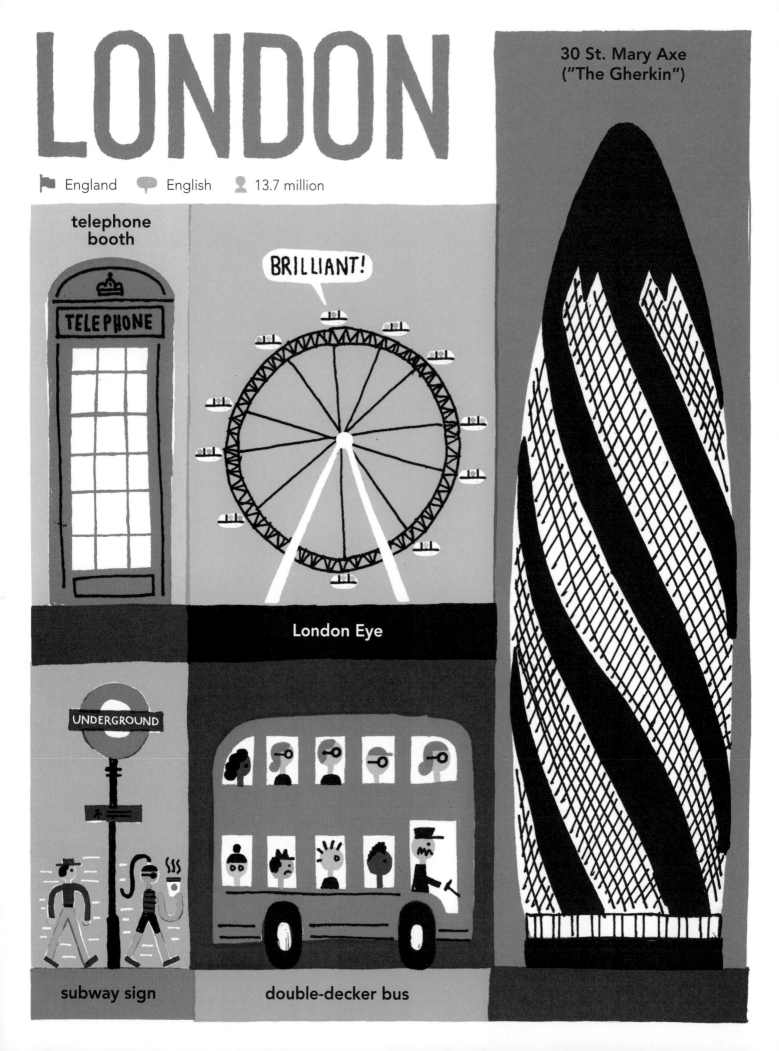

PARIS

France   French   12.4 million

newsstand

gendarme

baguette

Eiffel Tower

Arc de Triomphe

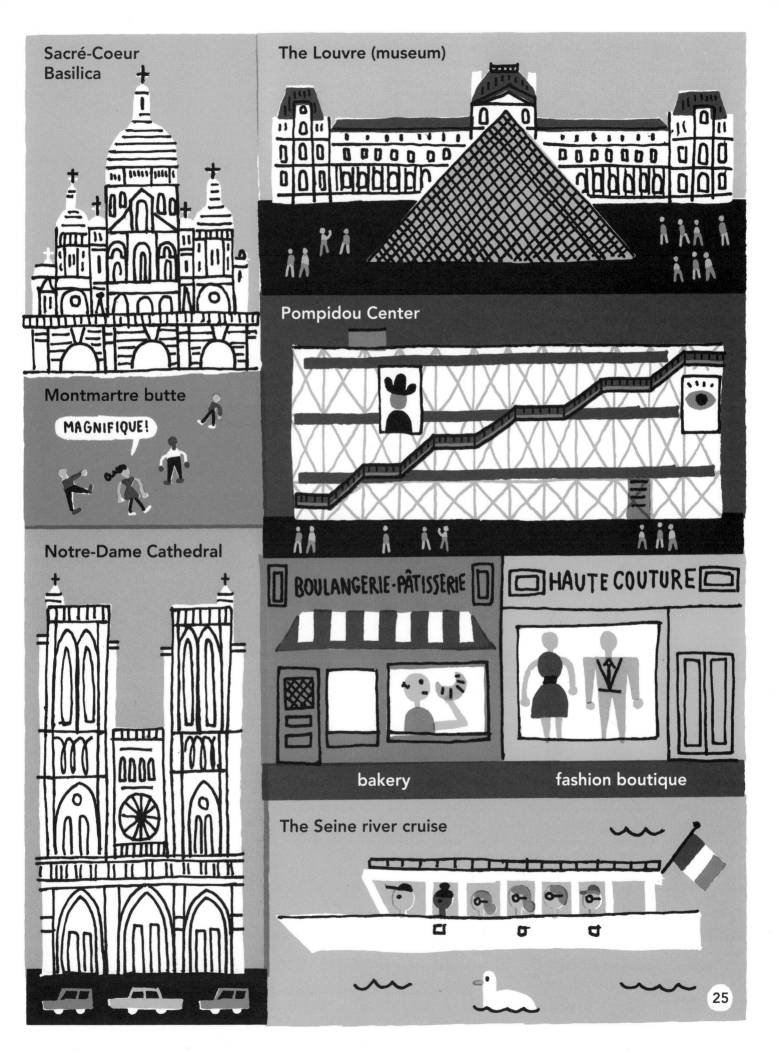

Sacré-Coeur Basilica

The Louvre (museum)

Montmartre butte

MAGNIFIQUE!

Pompidou Center

Notre-Dame Cathedral

BOULANGERIE-PÂTISSERIE

HAUTE COUTURE

bakery

fashion boutique

The Seine river cruise

25

AMSTERDAM

tulip

Netherlands   Dutch   1.1 million

Amsterdam Central railway station

De Gooyer windmill

brewery

cyclists

canal

stroopwafel (waffle with syrup)

26

tall, narrow buildings

Rembrandt, Van Gogh and Vermeer paintings at the Rijksmuseum

TO VONDELPARK, PLEASE!

bike taxi

star soccer player

patat oorlog

(fries with mayonnaise, onions and peanut sauce)

flower market

BERLIN

🏴 Germany   💬 German   👤 4.4 million

döner kebab

Berlin TV Tower

Reichstag (parliament building)

Buddy Bear painted statue

Brandenburg Gate

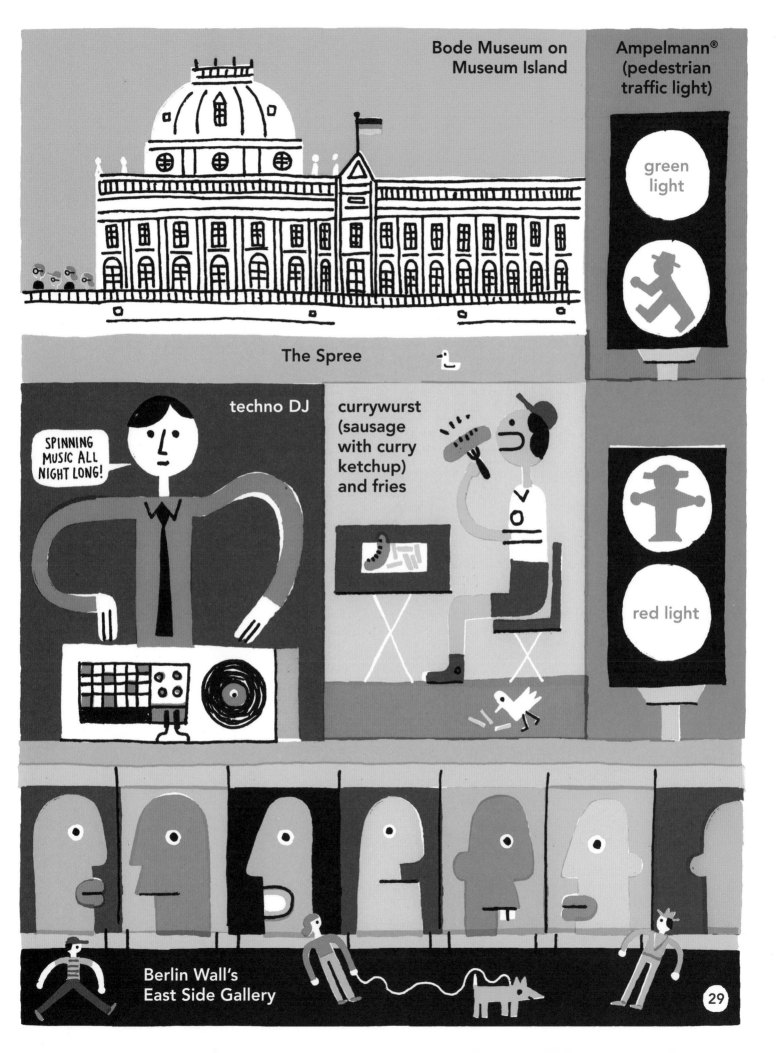

STOCKHOLM

🏴 Sweden 💬 Swedish 👤 2.2 million

Pippi Longstocking

Royal Palace

Royal Palace guard

Norrström river

City Hall

kanelbulle (cinnamon roll)

Lake Malar

30

Ericsson Globe
(sports arena)

SkyView
glass gondola

hot-air
balloon
ride

national
hockey team player

glass obelisk
in Sergels
torg square

salvaged seventeenth-century warship *Vasa*

colorful Gamla Stan
(Old Town)

(Vasa Museum of maritime history)

31

ZURICH

🚩 Switzerland   💬 Swiss German   👤 1.3 million

Grossmünster church

Opera House

Üetliberg mountain

Uto Kulm Hotel

Limmat River public bath

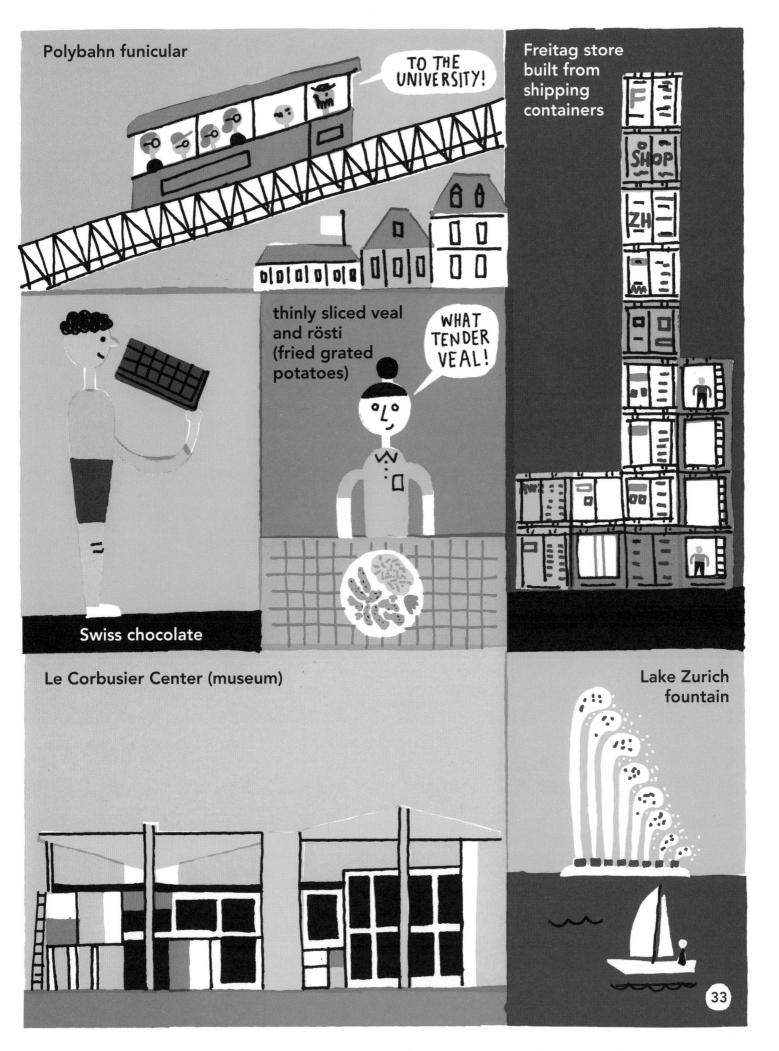

BARCELONA

🏳 Spain   💬 Spanish   👤 5 million

Joan Miró sculpture

champion soccer player

tapas (appetizers)

Sagrada Familia basilica

El drac fountain by Antoni Gaudi

(Park Güell)

Parc de la Ciutadella

Agbar Tower

Pablo Picasso painting

Magic Fountain of Montjuïc

Montserrat mountain (northwest of the city)

monastery

Barceloneta Beach

Mediterranean Sea

ROME

🏳 Italy   🗣 Italian   👤 4.3 million

Colosseum

gelato (Italian ice cream)

OUCH!

Mouth of Truth
(believed to bite a liar's hand)

Pantheon

36

motorino (scooter)

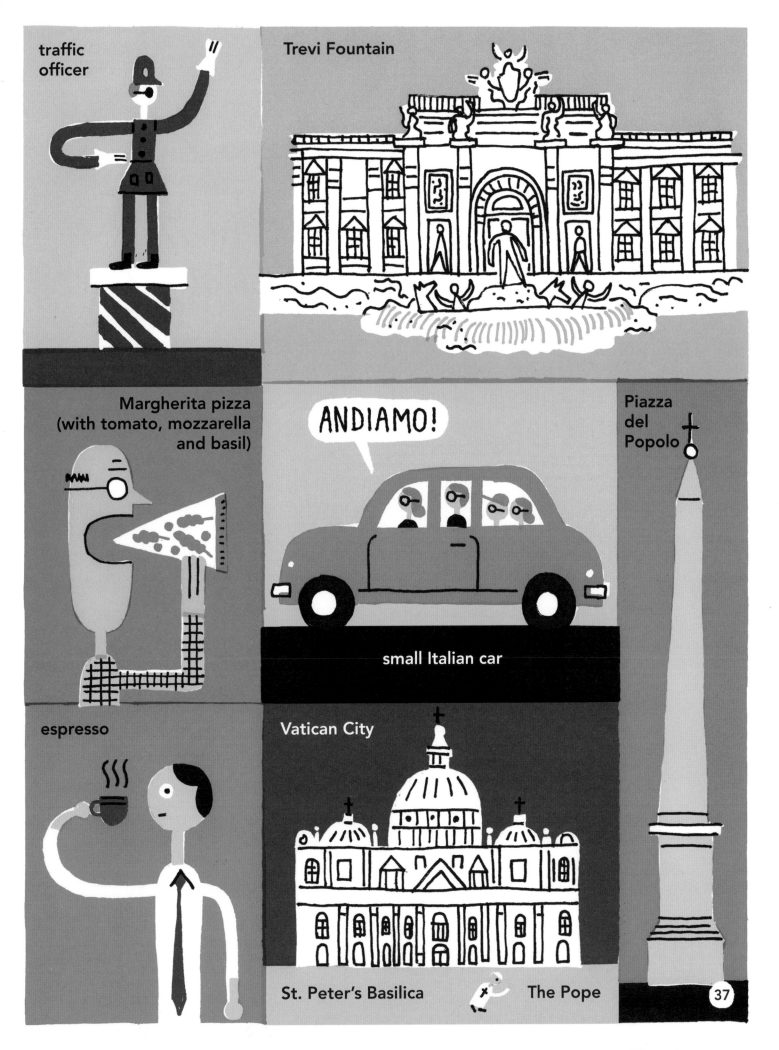

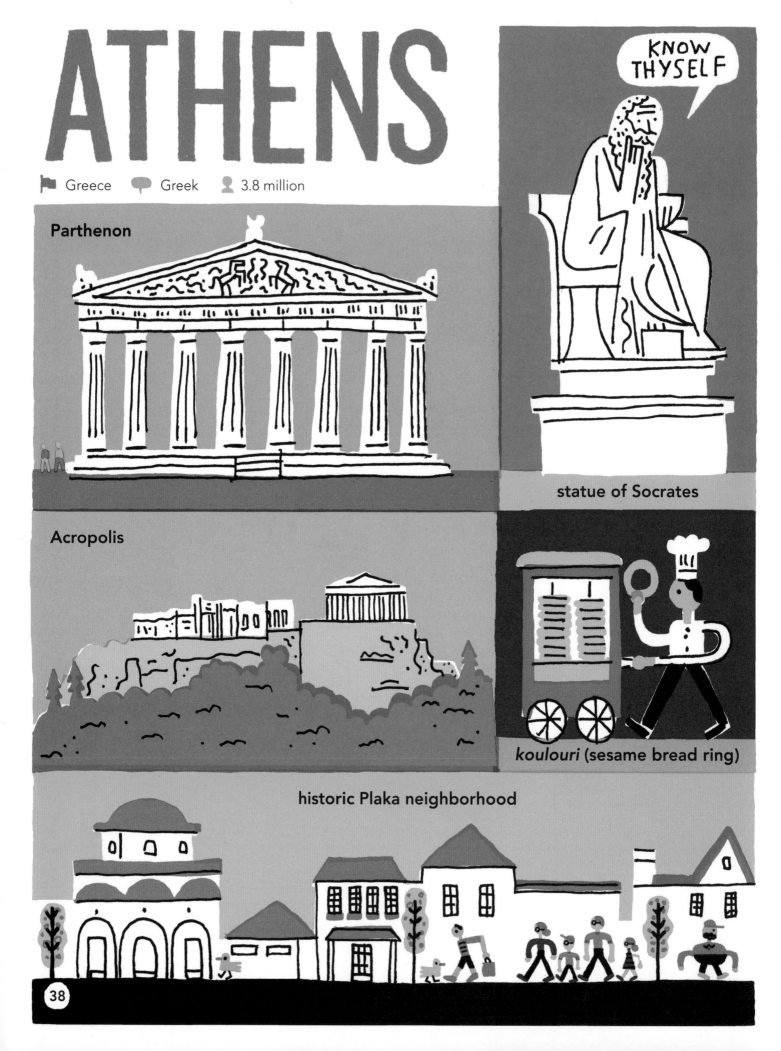

ATHENS

Greece · Greek · 3.8 million

Parthenon

Acropolis

KNOW THYSELF

statue of Socrates

koulouri (sesame bread ring)

historic Plaka neighborhood

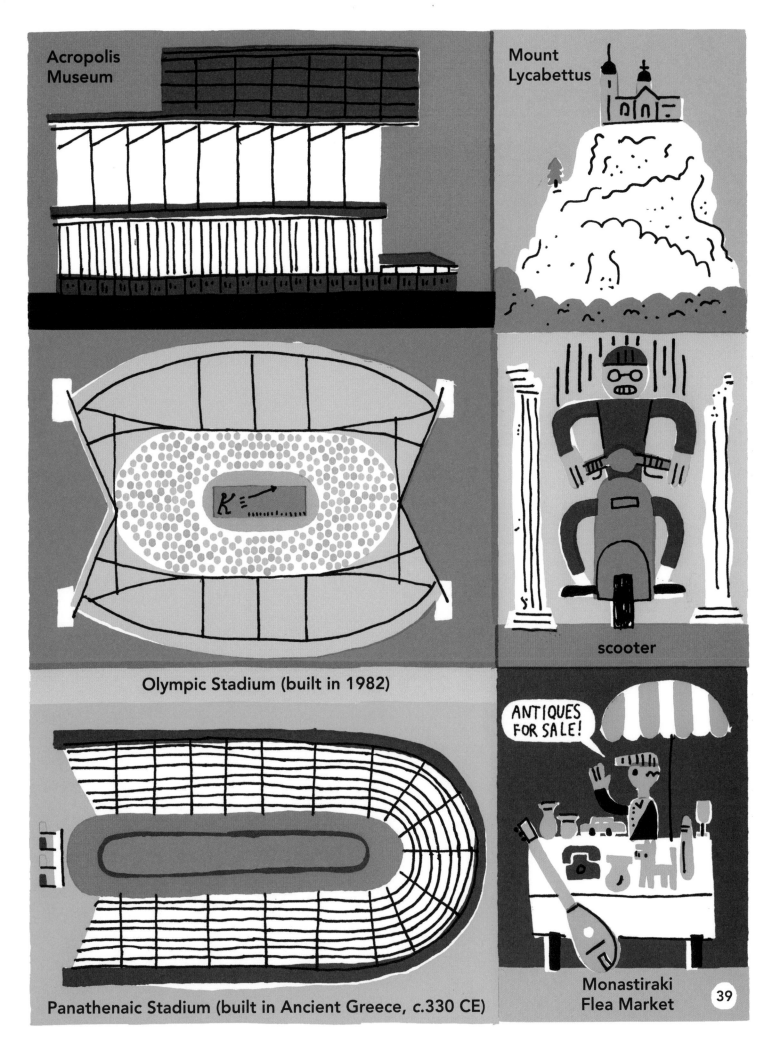

Acropolis Museum

Mount Lycabettus

Olympic Stadium (built in 1982)

scooter

Panathenaic Stadium (built in Ancient Greece, c.330 CE)

ANTIQUES FOR SALE!

Monastiraki Flea Market

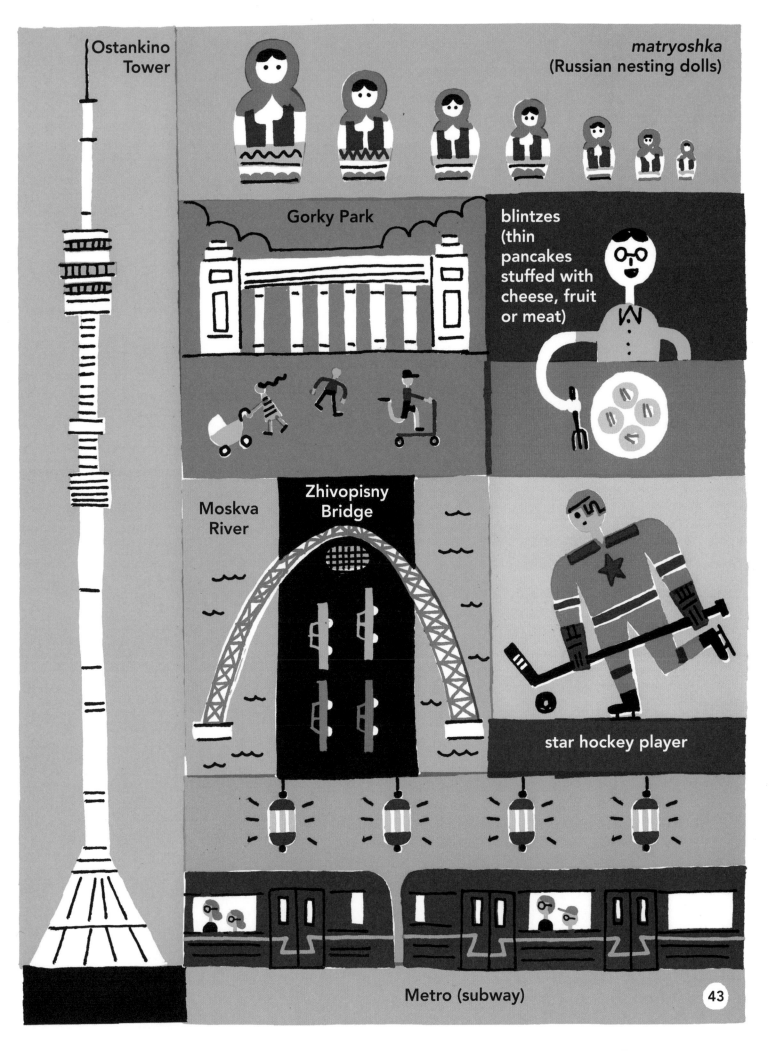

Ostankino Tower

matryoshka
(Russian nesting dolls)

Gorky Park

blintzes
(thin
pancakes
stuffed with
cheese, fruit
or meat)

Moskva River

Zhivopisny Bridge

star hockey player

Metro (subway)

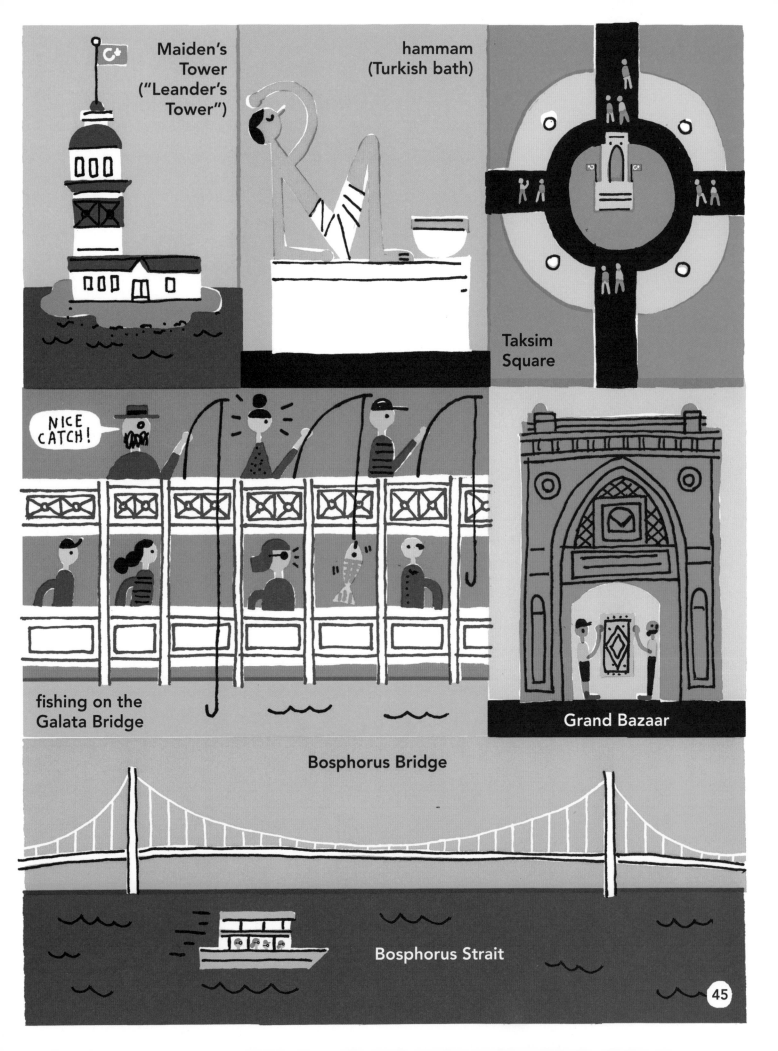

FEZ

Morocco   Arabic   1.2 million

couscous with meat or vegetables

Bab Boujeloud ("Blue Gate")

Medersa Bou Inania minaret

Dar el-Makhzen (royal palace)

medina (old town)

46

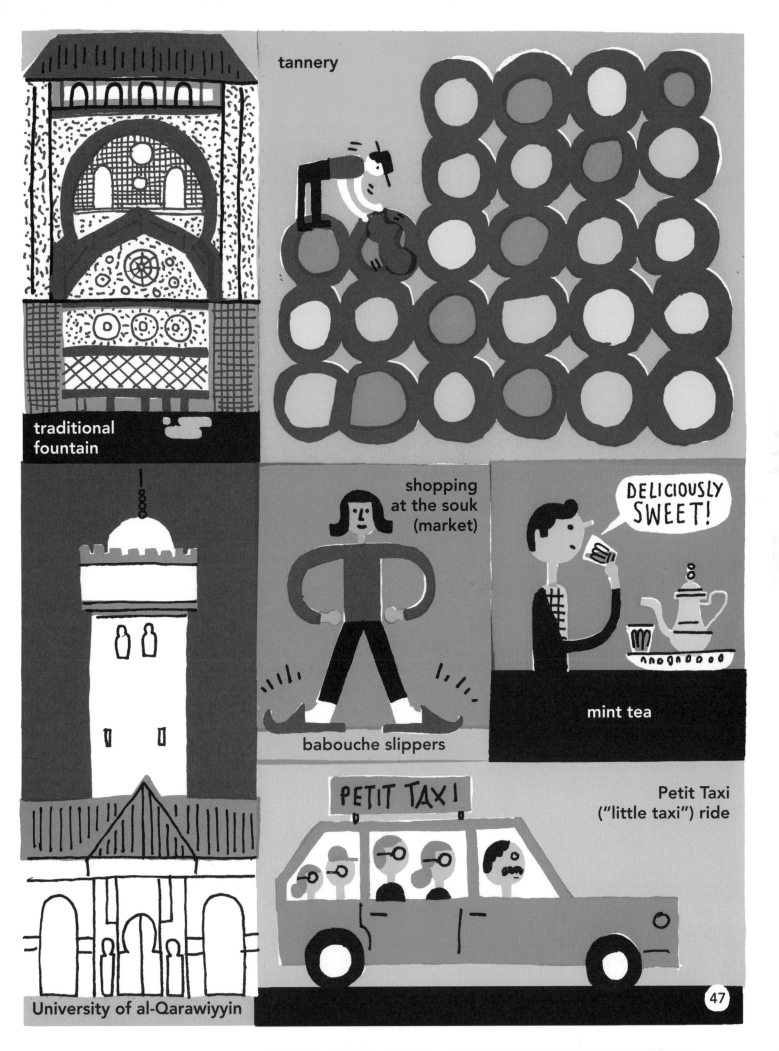

tannery

traditional fountain

shopping at the souk (market)

DELICIOUSLY SWEET!

mint tea

babouche slippers

Petit Taxi ("little taxi") ride

PETIT TAXI

University of al-Qarawiyyin

CAIRO

🏳 Egypt 💬 Egyptian Arabic 👤 20.4 million

Saladin
Citadel

Bab Zuweila gate

Al-Azhar
Mosque

kushari
(rice, macaroni, lentils
and fried onions)

Khan el-Khalili
souk (market)

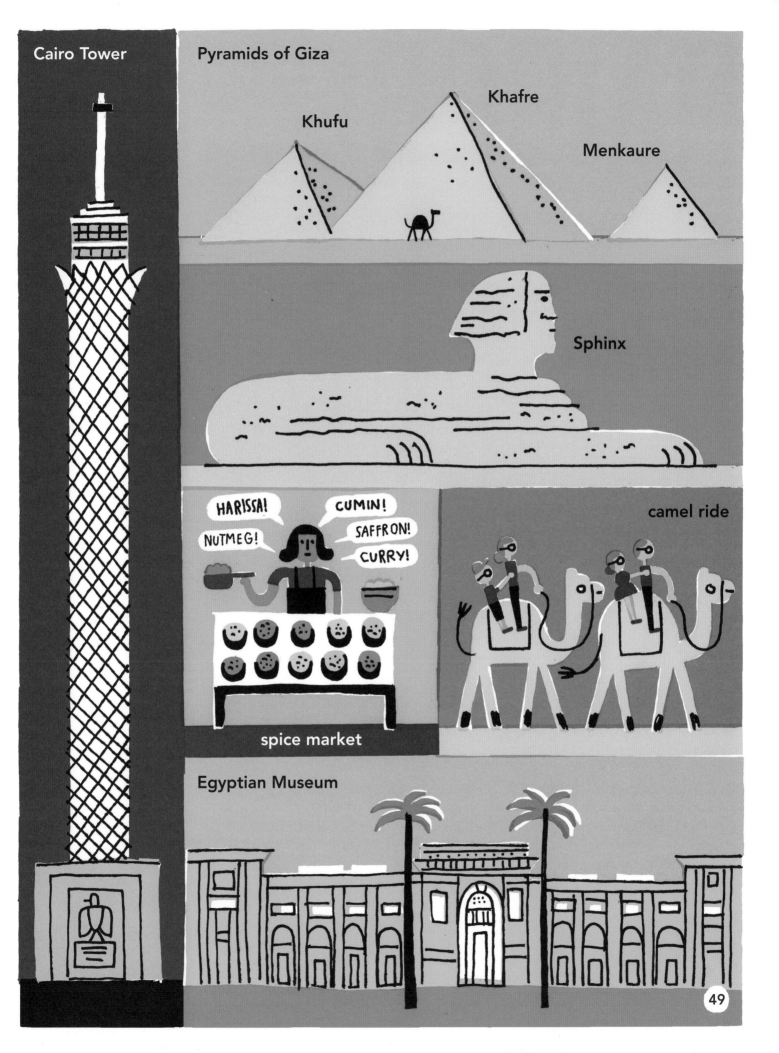

NAIROBI

🏴 Kenya 💬 Swahili, English 👤 4.5 million

Jamia Mosque

Uhuru Gardens

matatu (minibus) ride

chapati (flatbread)

sukuma wiki (collard greens)

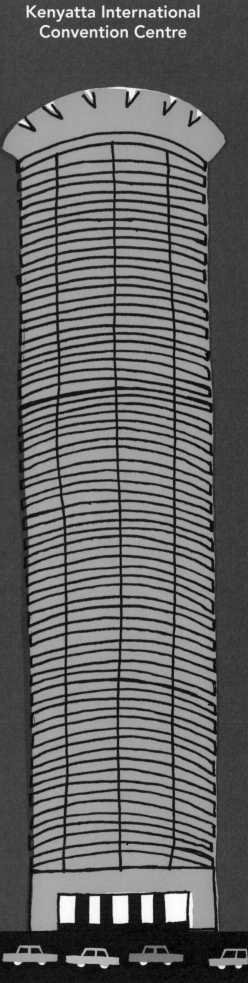

Kenyatta International Convention Centre

national park

giraffe sanctuary

wind farm on Ngong Hills
(southwest of the city)

Nyayo
Monument

dinosaur statue at the
National Museums of Kenya

WOW!

Maasai Market

JOHANNESBURG

South Africa   English, Sotho, Nguni and Afrikaans   4.4 million

Orlando Power Station towers

Soweto township

Nelson Mandela statue

WHAT A GRAND MAN!

Nelson Mandela Bridge

biltong (spiced dried meat)

rugby player

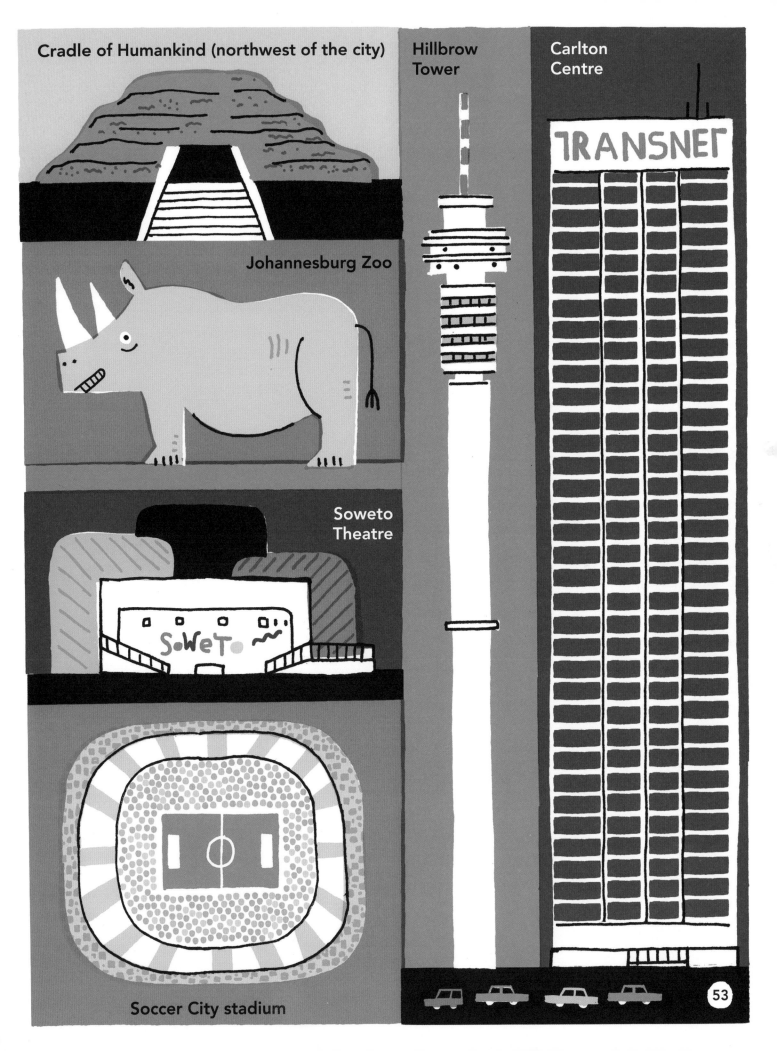

Cradle of Humankind (northwest of the city)

Hillbrow Tower

Carlton Centre

Johannesburg Zoo

Soweto Theatre

SOWETO

Soccer City stadium

TRANSNET

53

MUMBAI

India   Marathi   21.9 million

statue of Ganesh
(Hindu god)

Siddhivinayak Temple

VROOOM

auto rickshaw

Imperial
Towers

Haji Ali Dargah mosque

Haji Ali Bay

54

Gateway of India

dahi puri (pastry stuffed with potatoes and chickpeas)

DAHI PURI

Global Vipassana Pagoda

corn on the beach

Dharavi neighborhood

WELCOME

Elephanta Caves

HONG KONG

China · Cantonese, English · 9.6 million

Sik Sik Yuen Wong Tai Sin Temple

Clock Tower

traditional junk ship

modern ferry

harbor cruise

horse racing

GIDDY-UP!

Bank of China Tower

Lin Heung teahouse

Yuen Po Street Bird Garden

Bruce Lee statue on the Avenue of Stars

snake soup

Peak Tower

57

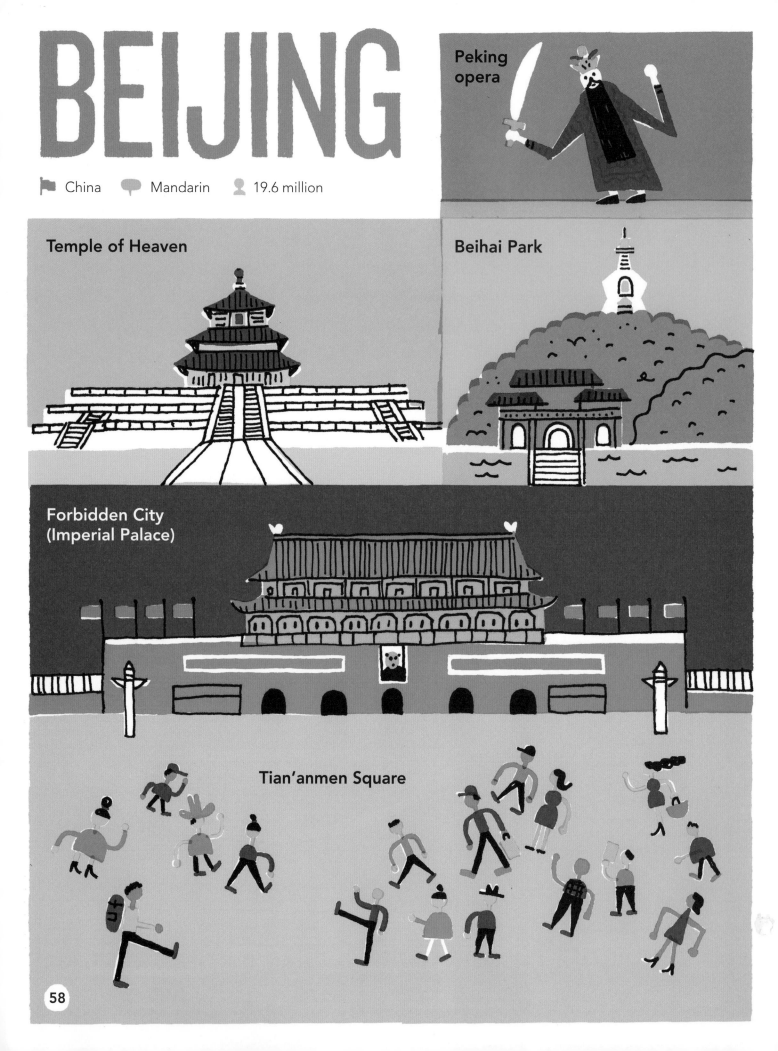

BEIJING

China · Mandarin · 19.6 million

Peking opera

Temple of Heaven

Beihai Park

Forbidden City (Imperial Palace)

Tian'anmen Square

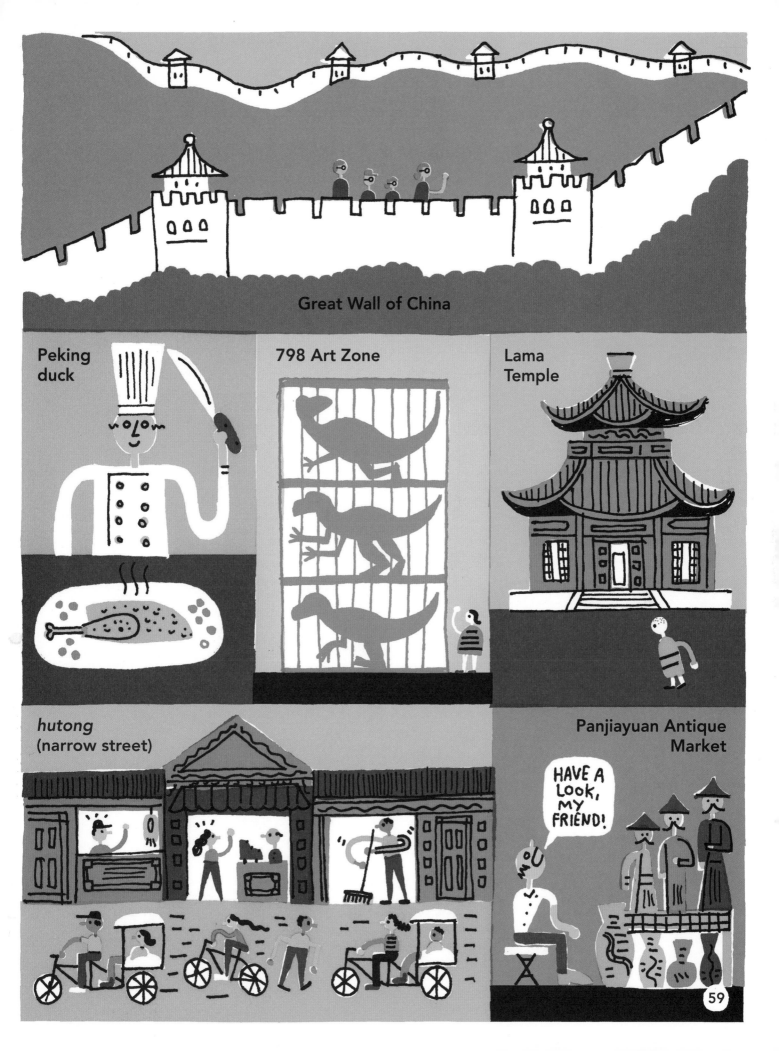

Great Wall of China

Peking duck

798 Art Zone

Lama Temple

hutong (narrow street)

Panjiayuan Antique Market

HAVE A LOOK, MY FRIEND!

TOKYO

🏴 Japan 💬 Japanese 👤 42.8 million

baseball player

Tokyo Tower

Mount Fuji

ramen (noodle soup)

karaoke

Shinjuku Gyoen National Garden

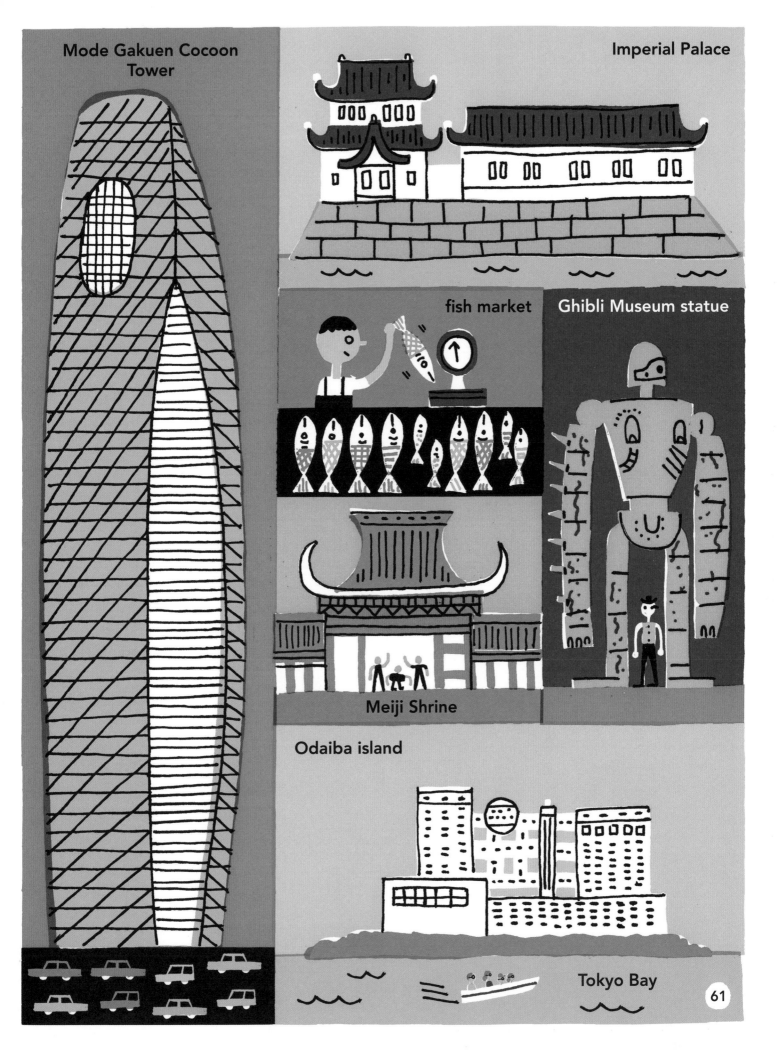

Mode Gakuen Cocoon Tower

Imperial Palace

fish market

Ghibli Museum statue

Meiji Shrine

Odaiba island

Tokyo Bay

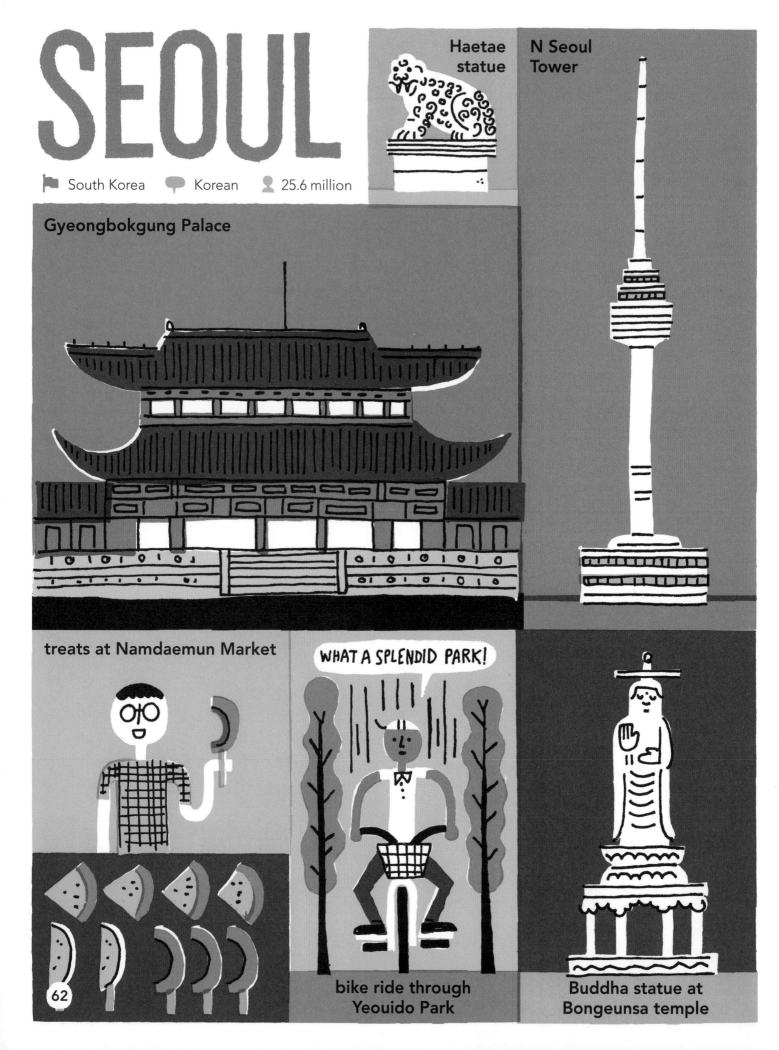

SEOUL

South Korea   Korean   25.6 million

Haetae statue

N Seoul Tower

Gyeongbokgung Palace

treats at Namdaemun Market

WHAT A SPLENDID PARK!

bike ride through Yeouido Park

Buddha statue at Bongeunsa temple

62

IFC skyscraper

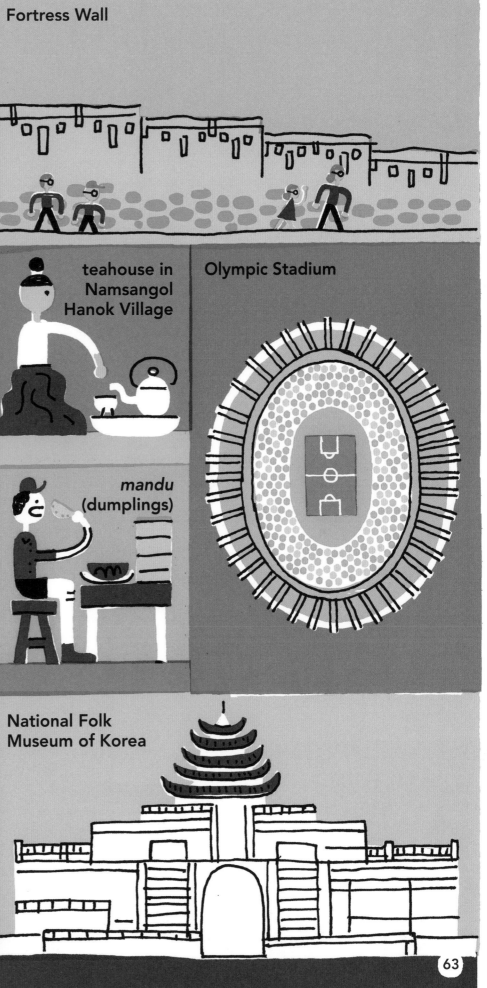

Fortress Wall

teahouse in Namsangol Hanok Village

Olympic Stadium

mandu (dumplings)

National Folk Museum of Korea

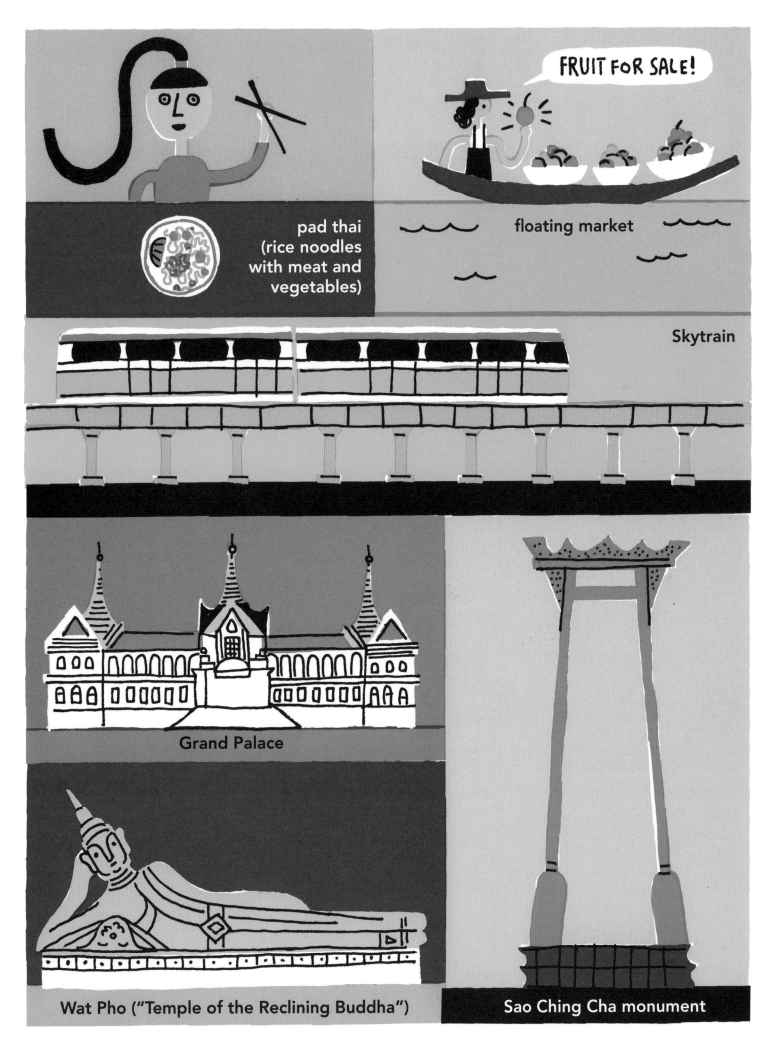

pad thai (rice noodles with meat and vegetables)

FRUIT FOR SALE!

floating market

Skytrain

Grand Palace

Wat Pho ("Temple of the Reclining Buddha")

Sao Ching Cha monument

JAKARTA

Indonesia   Indonesian   30.3 million

Istiqlal Mosque

Taman Mini park

gado-gado (salad with peanut sauce)

National Monument

drawbridge in the old town

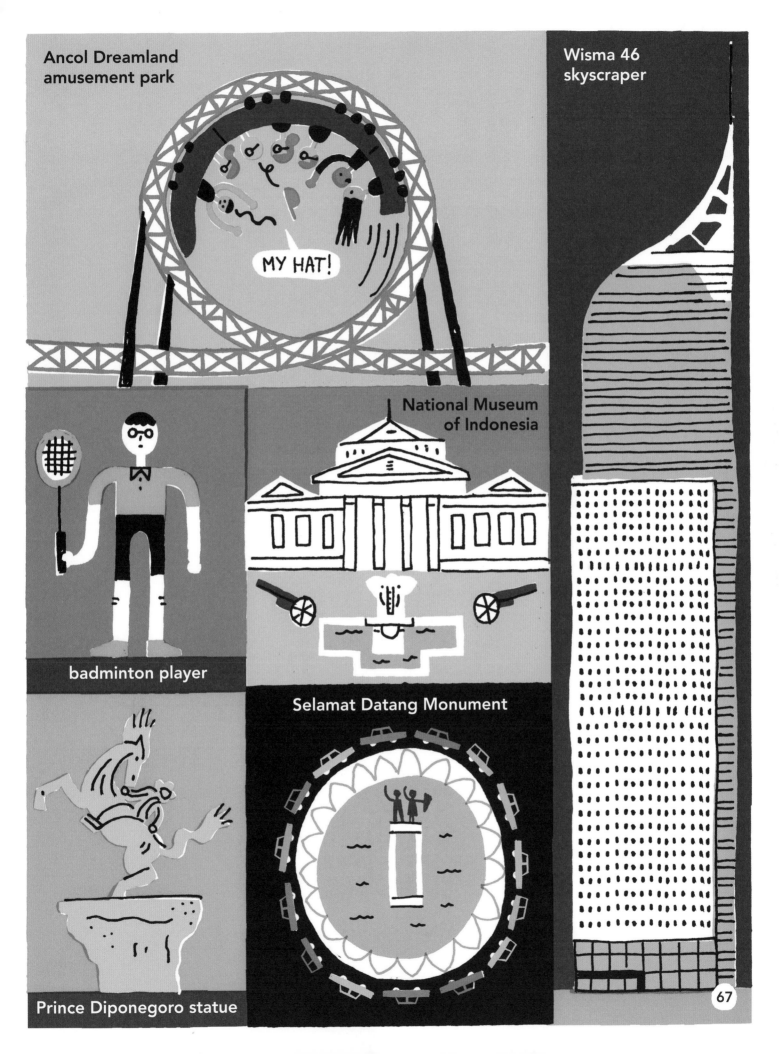

SYDNEY

🏳 Australia   💬 English   👤 4.7 million

kookaburra

SYDNEY IS MY FAVORITE CITY!

Sydney Harbour Bridge

Sydney Opera House

Port Jackson

boating in Sydney Harbour

Sydney Tower

city hall

lamington (cake coated in chocolate and coconut)

duck-billed platypus

Royal Botanic Gardens

surfing at Bondi Beach

SURF'S UP!

Woolloomooloo Bay

69

GLOSSARY

page 4   *bagel chaud; au four à bois* (French):
          hot bagels; from wood-fired oven

page 17   *es picante* (Spanish): it's spicy

page 18   *gigantesco* (Portuguese): gigantic

page 20   *mi amor* (Spanish): my love

page 25   *magnifique* (French): magnificent
          boulangerie (French): bakery
          pâtisserie (French): pastry shop
          haute couture (French): high fashion

page 37   *andiamo* (Italian): let's go

For Catherine

This edition published by Kids Can Press in 2016

Originally published in French under the title *Metropolis* by Comme des géants inc.

Copyright © 2015 Benoit Tardif
Copyright © 2015 Comme des géants inc.
Translation rights arranged through the VeroK Agency, Barcelona, Spain

English translation © 2016 Kids Can Press

London:

🚇 ® Transport for London
Reproduced by kind permission of Transport for London.

Berlin:

The Ampelmann is a registered trademark of AMPELMANN GmbH, www.ampelmann.de.

Stockholm:

The image of Pippi Longstocking is a rendering of Astrid Lindgren's original character © Astrid Lindgren / Saltkråkan AB, the Astrid Lindgren Company.

Kids Can Press acknowledges the financial support of the Government of Ontario, through the Ontario Media Development Corporation's Ontario Book Initiative; the Ontario Arts Council; the Canada Council for the Arts; and the Government of Canada, through the CBF, for our publishing activity.

Published in Canada by
Kids Can Press Ltd.
25 Dockside Drive
Toronto, ON M5A 0B5

Published in the U.S. by
Kids Can Press Ltd.
2250 Military Road
Tonawanda, NY 14150

www.kidscanpress.com

Original edition edited by Nadine Robert
English edition edited by Katie Scott
Designed by Mathieu Lavoie

Manufactured in Shenzhen, China, in 3/2016 through Asia Pacific Offset.

CM 16 0 9 8 7 6 5 4 3 2 1

Library and Archives Canada Cataloguing in Publication

Tardif, Benoit, 1983–
[Metropolis. English]
    Metropolis / written and illustrated by Benoit Tardif.

Translation of: Metropolis.
For ages 4–8.
ISBN 978-1-77138-721-7 (bound)

    1. Cities and towns — Juvenile literature. I. Title.
II. Title: Metropolis. English.

 HT152.T3713 2016   j307.76   C2015-907121-6

Kids Can Press is a *CORUS*™ Entertainment company

10 London,
England

11 Paris,
France

12 Amsterdam,
Netherlands

13 Zurich,
Switzerland

14 Berlin,
Germany

15 Krakow,
Poland

16 Stockholm,
Sweden

17 Moscow,
Russia

1 Vancouver,
Canada

2 Toronto,
Canada

3 Montreal,
Canada

4 New York,
United States of America

5 Chicago,
United States of America

6 San Francisco,
United States of America

7 Mexico City,
Mexico

8 Rio de Janeiro,
Brazil

9 Buenos Aires,
Argentina

22 Fez,
Morocco

23 Cairo,
Egypt

24 Nairobi,
Kenya

25 Johannesburg,
South Africa